MW00964868

Peggy's Letters

Jacqueline Halsey

ORCA BOOK PUBLISHERS

National Library of Canada Cataloguing in Publication Data
Halsey, Jacqueline, 1948-
Peggy's letters / Jacqueline Halsey.

(Orca young readers)
ISBN 1-55143-363-X

1. World War, 1939-1945—England—London—Juvenile fiction.
I. Title. II. Series.

PS8615.A3938P43 2005   jC813'.6   C2005-904614-7

First published in the United States, 2005
Library of Congress Control Number: 2005930965

Summary: In the devastation of London in WWII, a ten-year-old girl loses everything only to make a surprising new friend.

Free teachers' guide available at www.orcabook.com

Orca Book Publishers gratefully acknowledges the support for its publishing programs provided by the following agencies: the Government of Canada through the Book Publishing Industry Development Program (BPIDP), the Canada Council for the Arts, and the British Columbia Arts Council.

Typesetting and cover design by Lynn O'Rourke
Cover & interior illustrations by Susan Reilly

In Canada:
Orca Book Publishers
Box 5626 Stn. B
Victoria, BC Canada
V8R 6S4

In the United States:
Orca Book Publishers
PO Box 468
Custer, WA USA
98240-0468

www.orcabook.com
Printed and bound in Canada.
08 07 06 05 • 6 5 4 3 2 1

For Mum.
And for children living in war
zones around the world.

A heartfelt thank-you to
everyone who helped make a
dream come true.

Chapter 1

News travels fast on our street. It flies over garden fences and zings along washing lines.

"Cooooeeee…Peggy luv. Run and tell your mum, Keddy's got sausages, one per ration book. But hurry, dear. There'll be ever such a long queue."

"Mum…Mum…There's sausages."

"I heard," calls Mum from the back door. "Thanks for letting us know, Mrs. P."

Pulling on my coat, I grab the strings of our gas-mask boxes and hurry into the kitchen. Last week the greengrocer had oranges in, but we were too late, and they were gone by the time it was our turn.

"Pee-hew, Tommy." I hold my nose and he copies me. He's so funny.

"It's no good. I'm going to have to change him," says Mum.

"But we'll be too late again."

Mum gives me a stop-whining look, and I know we're not going anywhere until my baby brother's in a clean nappy.

At last he's ready. I clip the straps of his harness to each side of the pram, and off we go, down the hill to the high street.

My friend Nora is skipping on the other side of the road.

"Keddy's got sausages," I yell.

"Mum's already in the queue," she yells back. "Come and call for me this afternoon. Bring your skipping rope."

"Right-oh."

A bit farther along we bump into the postman.

"Nothing for you today, Peggy," he says.

I sigh and bend down to stroke the air-raid warden's ginger cat.

"Keddy's got sausages," I purr.

"Don't dawdle, there's a luv," calls Mum.

The queue outside Keddy's butcher shop stretches all the way along the high street to the bomb-damaged house with the missing wall. I can see the wallpaper in the different rooms, just like a doll's house. We join the end of the line. It's going to be another long, long wait.

"What a lovely boy you are," coos the woman in front of us, patting Tommy on the head.

"He's only seventeen months old, but he's really smart," I tell her.

"I'm sure he is," says the woman, laughing and tickling Tommy under the chin. She and Mum start grumbling about the weather and the war and how the caterpillars ate most of the cabbages. I'm bored with listening, so I twirl Tommy's pram beads and make him giggle.

The queue shuffles up to the butcher's shop window.

"Nearly our turn," says Mum.

At last I see the circle of sausages. Tonight they'll be sizzling in our frying pan. Mmmmm. I can almost taste them.

3

Tommy claps his hands over his ears, and before I can say, "What's the matter?" I hear the whistling shriek of a Doodlebug too.

Mr. Keddy runs out of his shop waving his arms. "In here," he yells. "Quick everybody."

"Go on, Peggy," shouts Mum as she gets Tommy out of his pram.

I want to stay with Mum, but she nudges me forward, so I follow the other customers to the back of the shop and down the steps into the cellar. There's sawdust on the floor, and it smells of blood. My legs turn to jelly, and my heart feels like it's going to jump out of my body. Mum pushes her way through and stands next to me. Tommy is screaming at the top of his lungs, but I can still hear the bomb's whine over all his noise. I know when the engine stops it will fall out of the sky and explode on whatever's below.

"Don't fall on us today. Don't fall on us today." I chant the magic words under my breath. They always keep me safe.

"I hate Doodlebugs," says Mum. "They're worse than the Blitz." Her lip trembles like she's going to cry. She cries a lot these days.

"There there, dear," says Mr. Keddy, patting Mum on the shoulder. "Stiff upper lip, girl, that's the way. Got to be brave in front of the kiddies."

Mum looks really frightened. I thought it was just kids that got scared. Tommy is still crying.

"There there, dear," I say. "Stiff upper lip, that's the way." My voice is all shaky. It doesn't sound like me at all, and Tommy's lips are wobblier than ever. But I know how to make him laugh.

"Look, Tommy." I uncurl his fingers and tickle his hand. "Round and round the garden, like a teddy bear. One step." Tommy watches my fingers marching up his arm.

The cellar is quiet now that Tommy has stopped crying. "Two steps..."

Why am I the only one talking? Looking up, I see frightened eyes all around me.

"Mum!" I cry. "I can't hear the bomb anymore."

There's a loud crack, and a rumble of thuds shakes the floor. Flakes of plaster and dust flutter down on us like snow.

No one moves.

"Tiggle," says Tommy.

"Oh, Tommy! Tickle you under there."

Tommy bursts into giggles, and we all breathe again. We're laughing. We're safe. I hug Tommy tight, and Mum hugs us both.

"Cor blimey! Bit too close for comfort, that one," says Mr. Keddy, wiping his forehead with his handkerchief. He pulls out a barley sugar and gives it to me. I stare at it. Sweets are rationed.

"Go on, take it," he says.

I pop the sweet in my mouth and mumble a sticky thank-you.

At last the single note of the all-clear siren sounds, and we climb up into the daylight. The shop window is a spider's web of cracks.

"Could be worse," says Mr. Keddy with a sigh. "Now who was next in line?"

Outside there's dust and smoke and something really strange. The tree in front of the butcher's shop is covered with dresses, all waving their sleeves in the breeze.

People are everywhere.

"Three of 'em nasty rocket bombs came over at once," I hear someone say.

"Poor Miss Rose," says another. "Looks like her shop took a direct hit."

"Give us a hand, Peggy," calls Mum. "I've got our sausages."

After clipping Tommy into the pram and packing the sausages at his feet, we start for home. A fire engine races by. It's going in our direction.

"Ding, ding, ding," says Tommy, ringing a pretend fire-engine bell.

Just as we get to the corner, Nora races up.

"Peggy, you've got to come quick. Your house got hit!"

Chapter 2

Mum and I start running at the exact same moment, bumping Tommy up and down in the pram as we go. Nora runs alongside.

Our house is in flames.

"Stand back there!" cries the fire chief.

"But it's our house."

"Is that right, missus?"

Mum nods.

"Sorry to hear that, luv." He turns to the small crowd that's forming. "Stand back. Let my men do their job." With out-spread arms, he herds everyone onto the far curb.

I watch the flames eat our house. The roof has fallen in, and the front wall is down. Now everyone can see our home in its underwear. The neighbors pat me on the shoulder, then talk as if I'm not there.

"Blinkin' war."

"Lucky escape."

"Poor dears."

Their pity is almost worse than the fire.

There's a gasp. Another wall crumples to the ground. Nora puts her arm round me. She is talking, but her words are snatched away with the sparks and the smoke. I can only hear the fire. A cup of tea grows cold in my hands. I don't even know how it got there.

The gray sky darkens into night. The fire is out. Everyone goes. Even Nora says good-bye. I picture families in their homes, putting up the blackouts, making supper and listening to the wireless. I want to go home too.

"Come on, dears," says a Red Cross lady. "Nothing more you can do here. They've

set up a rest center in St. Mark's church hall. If you've nowhere else to go, you can spend the night there."

I don't want to go. This is our home.

"Come back in the morning. Sort things out then." She turns to a short woman with bouncy chins. "Maud, can you take them along to St. Mark's?"

"Course I can," says Maud, taking Mum firmly by the arm. She ushers her along while I follow behind, pushing Tommy in the pram.

The church hall seems very bright after the blackness of the street. Maud sits us down at a long table and brings over soup and sandwiches. I swirl my soup into a whirlpool. Mum's messing with hers too. Only Tommy tucks in.

"You enjoy your supper while I set up some beds," says Maud. "Poor dears, you look tuckered out."

I'm not hungry, but we never waste food these days, so I start eating. I wish Maud would stop calling me a "poor dear."

11

"All finished?" says Maud a bit later. "I'll show you where I've put you for the night." She leads us to a corner that smells of old hymnbooks, then bustles off.

"As long as we are all together," says Mum, sitting on one of the beds. "That's all that matters..." Her voice cracks and fades away. She pulls Tommy onto her knee and rocks him.

I take out my notebook. It's the only paper I have to write to Dad.

Dear Dad

I can't believe everything's gone. Not just the house and all the things we need, but our special things too. Mum's lost our photos, and I've lost my biscuit tin of your letters. It was my most treasured possession in the whole world.

Tonight, home is a musty old church hall. There are other families living here too. Will this be our home until the war is over?

The question sits inside me like a big cold lump.

Little kids are racing about, and a sing-along has started round the piano. How can they act like everything's normal?

Love, Peggy

Tommy's asleep at last. A queue forms for the lav. The lights dim. Mum and I lie down in our clothes. Perhaps if I close my eyes I can pretend I'm back in my own bedroom. I imagine the blue flowery bedspread with Old Bear sitting on my pillow. But it's no use. The pictures in my head are of angry flames destroying everything. In the darkness I can hear people coughing and sniffing, wriggling and snoring. Someone near me is sobbing quietly. I suddenly realize it's Mum.

Chapter 3

I'm awake. If I don't open my eyes, yesterday may have been a bad dream.

"Morning all," says a cheery voice. "Looks like it's going to turn out nice. Bit chilly, mind you."

No use pretending any longer. That's Maud's voice, and I'm lying on an uncomfortable camp bed in a drafty church hall.

"Hello, Maud. I didn't see you there," says Mum. Her voice is tired, and her eyes are puffy.

Around us, the church hall bustles with people getting ready for the day. Beds are being packed up, blankets folded. Tommy's fussing.

"What are we going to do, Mum?"

"Have breakfast," interrupts Maud. "Can't go making decisions on an empty stomach. There's toast and jam over there. You'll get a nice cuppa tea too." Maud moves on to the next family.

"Mum?"

"I don't know, luv. I really don't know."

Tommy jumps into my arms.

"Oooo, he's soaking wet."

"Peggy, luv, everything we own is in the pram. There are no more nappies." She buries her face in her hands.

"Well, you can't stay like this, Tommy. Hold your arms up. Let's get all these soggy clothes off you." I pat him dry with the pram sheet, fold it into a triangle and pin it round his bottom.

"You'll have to wear your outdoor coat indoors today. It's a let's-be-silly day."

Tommy wriggles down onto the floor and scampers around.

"What would Dad do?"

15

"Let's go and have breakfast," says Mum, without answering my question.

By the time we have finished eating, Tommy's face, hands, hair and coat are covered in blackberry jam, but at least Mum looks better.

"Do you think you could stay here and watch your brother for me?" she asks as we clean him up and rinse out his clothes.

"I'll keep an eye on them for you, dear," calls Maud from behind the tea urn.

"I don't need anyone keeping an eye on me," I whisper loudly to Mum.

Maud hears and laughs. "Course you don't. But I'll be here anyway."

I wish Maud would go away.

"Where are you going, Mum?"

"I've got to see someone about tonight."

"Can't we come too? Please don't make me stay here on my own."

"It's better if I go by myself, Peggy. Won't be long, I promise."

I look around the hall, then back at Mum. "Okay."

"That's my girl." We both smile at Dad's favorite expression.

"Keep your fingers crossed for me," she says, tying a scarf around her head and pulling on her coat. "Be a good boy, Tommy."

After Mum leaves I hold Tommy's hand, and we toddle slowly round the church hall, ending up at the piano. I lift him onto the wide stool, and he pounds away on the yellow keys. A woman joins us with her little boy, and the two of them begin a deafening duet.

Why isn't Mum back yet? She's been gone ages. A panicky feeling twists my insides into knots. Supposing she doesn't come back. The door squeaks. I look up. But it's not Mum. It's a scruffy-looking boy trying to get my pram out of the door.

"Stop!"

The pram is stuck half in and half out. I race over and grab the handle.

"Let go."

"Keep your hair on. I'm not nicking it. I'm going to bring it back," says the boy.

17

I don't like his attitude.

"You don't borrow things without asking."

"Weren't no one to ask, Miss Bossy Boots."

"My name's Peggy. What do you want my pram for anyway?"

The boy pushes a scraggly ginger curl out of his eyes.

"I found something really big to add to my shrapnel collection. I thought the caretaker's trolley would be around, but I can't find it. Let me use your pram. You can come with me if you like."

"What makes you think I want some dirty old bit of metal in my pram? Anyway, I've got to look after my little brother."

"Aww, come on. It's only just up the road."

Sunshine is squeezing through the half-opened door, and I long to get out of the smelly church hall. I look back at Tommy. He's playing happily with the other little boy. Maud is there too, and she did offer to keep an eye on us.

"All right," I say. "Just for a minute. Hold the door open."

I steer the pram through the narrow gap and bump it down the steps.

"What's your name?"

"Stanley, but everyone calls me Spud," he says, taking the handle of the pram. After a few steps, Spud sticks his bottom out and walks along on his toes.

"Cootchie cootchie coo, little baby," he says in a squeaky, posh-lady voice. I start giggling. He looks so silly.

"You're daft."

Spud starts running with the pram, zigzagging on two wheels round everything in sight while making airplane noises. I fly along beside him.

"You're not daft; you're crazy."

Suddenly Spud spins the pram on its back wheels and screeches to a halt in front of a recently bombed house. Wisps of smoke are still rising from the ashes.

"Here we are," he says, abandoning the pram and me and taking off over a mountain of rubble.

I feel like I've turned into a statue.

"This is my house," I say in a croaky whisper.

Through a teary blur, I look at the black, soggy wreck. Our home is just another bomb site. Spud turns and points to a large triangle of metal sticking out of the remaining wall.

"Look," he calls, his eyes gleaming. "It's part of the tail fin of a V1 bomb."

"I don't want to look," I shout up at him. "This isn't a stupid game. This is my home." Spud turns back to his "find" and starts un-burying it before I've even finished talking. I swing the pram round, nearly knocking Mum off the pavement.

"Mum!"

Chapter 4

"Peggy! What's happened? Where's Tommy?" Mum's voice is almost a scream. "Where is he?"

"Nothing's happened. Tommy's back at the hall. Oh, Mum, look at our house." I burst into tears.

Mum stops being angry and wraps me in her arms. "Poor house," she says softly.

She undoes her hug and pulls out a handkerchief. "Now dry those tears and have a blow. You were supposed to stay in the hall and look after Tommy."

"I only meant to go out for a minute. Just to get some air. I didn't know I was coming here." Tears pour out of my eyes.

"There, there, that's enough crying."

"But I cccccan't stoppppp," I say through hiccupy sobs. "I might have to crrry forever."

"I know," says Mum, hugging me again. "I feel like that too sometimes."

As we turn back toward St. Mark's, the ginger cat appears from behind a pile of broken bricks and purrs round my ankles. I scratch him behind his ears. "Glad you're safe, Puss."

"Come on. Let's get back to Tommy," says Mum.

I'm wheeling the pram, but her arm is still round my shoulders.

"What I don't understand is why you brought the pram with you in the first place," she says as we walk along.

"That boy wanted to borrow it," I explain, turning to point at Spud, who has been joined by several other boys. He's so busy digging in the rubble he doesn't notice us leaving. "He thinks our house is a playground. We must stop him, Mum."

"No," says Mum. "It's time for us to think about what we're going to do next. I've been to see Grandad. He says we can stay with him for a while."

"Stay at Grandad's!" My memory of Grandad is a tall grumpy man in a black suit. "I don't think he likes us."

"Of course he likes you."

"Then why doesn't he ever come and see us?"

"I don't know. Dad's his only son, but they never got on very well. I think he feels sad about that now."

"But if we live at Grandad's, I'll have to change schools. I won't see Nora."

A familiar yell pierces the air. We park the pram and race up the church hall steps.

"Oh, there you are," calls Maud. She's holding a red-faced, wriggling, screaming Tommy. They both look very cross.

Tommy leaps into my arms.

"Sorry about this," says Mum. "There was a bit of a misunderstanding."

While Maud goes on and on about how

irresponsible it was to leave without telling her, I take Tommy back to our corner.

Mum joins us a few minutes later. "Let's get our things together," she says.

There's not much to get together, just Tommy's damp clothes.

"Oh dear," says Mum. "Look at you two. Tommy's practically naked, and you look like you've been through a hedge backward. What will Grandad think if he sees you like this?"

I try smoothing the creases out of my crumpled dress, but it doesn't look much different.

Mum rummages in her handbag and pulls out a comb. "We can't do anything about our clothes, but I can do something with your hair."

It hurts to have the tangles combed out, but I like having Mum do my hair. It feels so normal. She braids two plaits and looks at her handiwork.

"You'll do," she says with a smile. "Now go and wash your face."

On my way back to Mum, Maud stops me. She seems to have got over her Tommy experience. A smile is back on her face, and a large brown paper bag is in her hands. "I managed to scrounge up a few nappies and some baby things," she says. "Give these to your mum.

"Maud, you're a lifesaver," calls Mum when she sees the contents of the bag. "This will tide us over nicely."

Together, we change Tommy's nappy, squeeze him into a romper suit a size too small, and button on a cardigan two sizes too big.

I twirl him round. "You look smashing, Tommy. Doesn't he, Mum?"

Tommy claps. Mum just shakes her head and tries to roll up his sleeves. "At least it's better than a coat and a nappy." She picks up the bag. "Time we made a move."

"Thanks for all your help, Maud," calls Mum, opening the door. She stops. "There's just one last thing."

"Yes, my dear."

"Do you know anyone who could use a pram? We won't have any room where we're going."

"No," I shout. "We're not leaving the pram."

"Look at it, Peggy. The wheels are wobbly, and all the metal bits are rusty. Anyway, Tommy's nearly grown out of it.

"But it's all we have left."

Mum sighs and along comes the pram.

Chapter 5

We take the train to Grandad's even though it's only two stops. Tommy loves trains, and the pram is able to go in the guard's van.

"Chuff chuff...whooo whooo," sings Tommy as we walk up from the station. No one says "hello" to me, and the only cat we pass scoots away into the bushes.

"Here we are," says Mum. "Railway Lane." We turn into a long street of narrow, joined-together houses. They all look exactly the same.

"Grandad's is number eighty-nine," says Mum.

I count off the house numbers in twos. Our steps seem to slow as we reach the eighties.

"Eighty-five, eighty-seven. Here it is, eighty-nine."

This is my new home. The paintwork is gray and so are the bricks. Dingy lace curtains droop across the windows. It doesn't feel like home.

The sun has gone in, and a gust of wind whips my skirt hem up over my bare knees.

"Go on, Peggy, knock on the door. It's too cold to be hanging around outside."

I knock, and we wait. Perhaps he's not in, I think hopefully.

Grandad opens the door. He's smaller than I remembered, and his hair is whiter. An old beige cardigan hangs loosely off his stooped shoulders. It reminds me of Tommy in his outfit. I want to reach over and roll up Grandad's sleeves.

"Hello, Grandad."

Grandad doesn't smile as he grunts back a hello.

"Say hello to Grandad, Tommy." Tommy ducks round the back of me and clutches my legs so I can't move. I know how he feels. I want to hide too.

"You'd best come in," says Grandad. Mum always says his bark is worse than his bite, and that is just how he sounds, like a grumpy old dog.

"What shall I do with the pram?" I whisper to Mum.

"Leave the blessed thing outside," she whispers back crossly. Then she turns to Grandad. "It's really good of you to put us up like this." She gives him a peck on the cheek.

Grandad growls again and mumbles something about duty and there being a war on.

"We'll take our coats upstairs. Then shall I put the kettle on and make us all a nice cup of tea?" asks Mum in her too cheery voice.

"Haven't got much milk. Hope you've brought your ration books" is Grandad's gruff reply.

I climb the narrow stairs with Tommy still glued to my leg.

A large bed, a narrow bed and a dressing table with a cracked mirror are all squeezed into the front bedroom. On the wall a cross-stitched sampler declares *Home Is Where the Heart Is*. Where is my heart?

"I'll sleep with Tommy," says Mum. "You take the little bed under the window."

I have to climb over the big bed to reach my bed. I plonk down on it. The bed has no bounce. Tommy thinks climbing from one bed to the other is the best game ever.

"Tommy's not going to like it here," I say, pulling him onto my lap. He wriggles free and leaps back onto Mum's bed.

Mum looks at me. Her eyes are serious, and her lips are thin and tight. She lowers her voice.

"Peggy, we've nowhere else to go. If Grandad won't have us, I don't know what we're going to do."

I didn't realize that this was only a maybe home.

31

"We're all going to have to try very hard to make this work. Don't race around, and don't touch anything. Try and be quiet..."

Mum's list of don'ts goes on and on.

"And most important of all," says Mum, "please help me watch Tommy. He's at a very busy stage."

"I'll try."

"Good girl. Let's go and put that kettle on." She catches Tommy. "Come on, young man. It's time you made friends with your grandfather."

"I'll be down in a minute, Mum." I take my notebook out of my coat pocket.

Dear Dad
It's so scary not belonging anywhere.

I can tell by Grandad's face that he doesn't want us to stay here for long. But if he turns us out, where will we go? Not back to Maud and the horrid church hall, I hope. I wish you were here. You'd work something out. I know you would.

Love, Peggy

Chapter 6

Grandad is sitting in the armchair, lighting his pipe, when I come into the room. I sit on the edge of my chair watching the blue circles of smoke curl up to the ceiling. The silence is louder than the tick of the mantelpiece clock.

A train goes by. Tommy scurries into the room and runs over to the window making *chuffa chuffa* noises.

Is this too much noise? I wonder. Should I make him be quiet? I look over at Grandad.

He takes his pipe out of his mouth. "I used to like trains when I was a boy," he says. "Just a blinkin' noisy nuisance now." He puffs more stinky smoke into the room.

Mum comes in with the tea. While we sip, Tommy takes off his shoe and chuffs it over the rug and under the table. His shoe-train is heading for Grandad's feet. I hold my breath. What's Grandad going to do?

At the last moment, Tommy's train changes direction and chuffs round the back of Grandad's chair. My breath comes out in a great whoosh.

Mum chatters, Grandad grunts, Tommy chuffs and I sit. The afternoon is as long as a wet week of Sundays, as my old teacher used to say.

At last the clock chimes five. Grandad levers himself out of his chair and limps over to the window. He pulls the blackout curtains across.

"Haven't much for tea," he mumbles.

My stomach is growling. I often feel hungry these days, and today we missed lunch. I jump up. "We've got sausages. They're in the bottom of the pram."

"Sausages!" says Grandad.

"I'd forgotten all about them," says Mum.

"There are some potatoes in the cellar," says Grandad. "And I can cut us a cabbage from the garden."

"Bubble and squeak and sausages. Yum!"

Soon the sausages are sizzling under the grill, and the potatoes and cabbage, mushed up into a hash, are turning golden brown in the frying pan. The kitchen smells delicious. Grandad gets the plates, and Mum has just finished serving up when the air-raid siren starts whining.

A cold shiver runs up my back. Please not this house too. I remember my chant—Don't fall on us today. Don't fall on us today—but the words have lost their magic.

"Move, girl. This way. Quick."

I suddenly realize that Grandad is talking to me.

"Quick," he says again. His forehead is

creased into a worried frown, and I see why. His air-raid shelter is a narrow bed in a reinforced cupboard under the stairs. It's made for one person.

"We can all fit in if we squish up really tight," I say, picking up Tommy.

"I'll stay out," says Grandad.

"No, look. Tommy, we're going to play sardines under the stairs. That means we have to squeeze in tight. Like this." I give him a bear hug. "Bubble, bubble, bubble." I carry him over to the cupboard and push him under the slanty part.

"Bub, bub, bub," says Tommy.

"Tommy, you're the best sardine I've ever seen." I slide in next to him. The ceiling is so low that I have to sit with my head on one side. Mum squishes up next to me, and there's just enough room for Grandad on the end.

"There, we all fit," says Mum.

My ears strain to catch the first drone of bomber planes or the sound of the ack-ack guns, but all I can hear is our breathing. The smell of sausages drifts into the under-the-stairs shelter. Our food is getting cold.

Is there time?

"Stay here, Tommy."

I duck out of the cupboard and make a dash for the kitchen.

"Come back," calls Mum.

"What do you think you're doing, girl? Get under the stairs!" yells Grandad.

I pick up two plates of dinner and carry them as fast and as carefully as I can back to Grandad and Mum.

Mum cheers. Tommy claps his hands.

"Good for you, girl," says Grandad.

I race back for my plate and Tommy's dish.

"We have sausages for tea, and it's going to take more than Mr. Hitler and his blinkin' bombs to stop us eating them," says Grandad.

I squeeze back into my space. Mum hands me a spoon so that I can feed Tommy. This is going to be messy.

Moments later the single note of the all-clear sounds. It was a false alarm.

Grandad moves to stand up. It's hard for him with his bad hip, but I don't think he'd like me giving him a boost.

"Tommy and I are going to finish our picnic here," I declare.

"Me too," says Mum.

"Well, I'd better stay as well," says Grandad, leaning back against the wall.

When he smiles, he looks like Dad.

"If you think about it, those sausages saved your lives," he says.

"Saved by a sausage," I announce with a giggle. Mum joins in. I feel cozy and safe. Maybe it's not going to be so bad living here after all.

Dear Dad

Mum said my under-the-stairs sausage picnic broke the ice, but I'm not sure. We've been at Grandad's for two weeks, and I can't seem to do anything without Grandad grumbling and Mum fussing.

Yesterday Mum picked up our utility coupons. We now have extra points to replace the clothes we lost. She thought we'd get the best deal down the market, so we spent a lovely morning looking at all the stalls. I now have a navy gymslip, a gray blouse and cardigan, two nighties and some underwear. Mum found herself a new dress. She looks really pretty in it. I still feel like a visitor. Being good is awfully hard work.

Tomorrow I start my new school. I wish Nora was coming with me.

Love, Peggy

Chapter 7

Mum finishes filling in the form and hands it back to Mrs. Mashman, the headmistress.

"We'd better go now," Mum says to me.

I'm hugging Tommy tight. I want them both to stay. Mum holds out her arms, and Tommy jumps into them. Babies are so lucky.

"See you this afternoon," I say in a small voice. "Bye, Tommy. Bye, Mum."

"Bye, luv."

"Good-bye, Mrs. Fisher," says the headmistress firmly.

Mum turns toward the door, and Mrs. Mashman turns toward me. Her beady eyes peer at me through thick round glasses.

"Follow me, Peggy Fisher. Your classroom is this way." She marches out of the office.

Through the window, I can see Mum and Tommy walking across the playground. I wave, but they have their backs to me so they don't wave back.

"Come along," calls Mrs. Mashman. "We haven't got all day."

I follow her down a long corridor to a noisy classroom. Mrs. Mashman flings open the door. There's instant silence.

"What is going on, Mrs. Bottomly?" she booms.

Mrs. Bottomly is a little old lady with snowy curls and bright pink cheeks.

"Everything is, is fine, Mrs. Mashman," she stammers. "Just some high spirits in class today."

The headmistress glares at both the class and the teacher. "Save your high spirits for the playground. This is Peggy Fisher, your new pupil."

I can feel the room staring at my mousy plaits, my snubby nose, my skinny legs and my uniform, which isn't quite the same as everyone else's. I want to crawl under Mrs. Bottomly's desk.

The headmistress turns on her heels and leaves the room. I stand rooted to the spot, listening to her footsteps echoing down the corridor. Nora would have said something funny, and the whole class would have instantly laughed and loved her. I just stand there looking at my shoes.

"Hang your coat and gas mask on the hook and sit next to Annie," says my new teacher, pointing to an empty desk. "Perhaps Annie can show you around at recess."

Annie is older than me and hardly gives me a glance before turning back to her friend. The classroom is getting noisy again.

"Settle down, children," says Mrs. Bottomly, fluttering her hands. "Let's get out our math books...No, stop that...Quiet now." Her pink cheeks get even pinker.

The room smells of chalk dust, just like my old classroom, but nothing else is the same. Instead of pictures on the walls, war posters tell everybody not to waste anything. The only books on the shelves are ratty old textbooks, nothing that looks fun to read.

An eraser flies across the room, then a piece of chalk. But no one seems to care. Out the window the playground waits for recess. My old playground had grass. This one is all concrete.

At last the bell rings, and the whole class runs for the door in a swirling mass of shrieks. Mrs. Bottomly straightens her books, takes off her glasses and, with a gasp, leaves the classroom too.

Annie doesn't stay behind to show me around. No one does.

I grab my coat and find my own way outside, where I wander round the hop-scotch squares and marble games alone. Mrs. Mashman is at her office window, watching the playground like a hawk. A football flies over and hits me on the leg.

"Ouch."

"Give us our ball back."

Oh, no. It's that Spud boy. What's he doing here? He looks different from the last time I saw him. His clothes are neat, and his curls are plastered down with grease.

"Hello, Peg," he says, looking as surprised as I am.

"My name's Peggy, and your ball's over there."

I turn my back on him. Why is the only person who talks to me someone I don't want to talk to, ever? I walk away and end up leaning against a wall, watching the skippers. Annie and another girl are turning a long length of rope. As it thwacks the ground, I automatically sway in rhythm, getting ready for the perfect moment to run in.

"I like coffee, I like tea. I want Doreen to jump in with me," chants one of the girls.

I ache to join in, but no one calls out my name.

44

Dear Dad

I am invisible. I really am. It only happens at school. As soon as I go through the gate, poof—no one can see me. I have been at this school for one whole week, and it happens every day.

I've looked in every girl's face to see who I would like for a friend. Nobody looks at me. Don't they know I'd be a very nice friend if only they would give me a try?

Love, Peggy

Chapter 8

I am sick. I have a cough, a stomach-ache, an earache and a sore foot. Mum still makes me go to school, off to another Monday sitting next to snooty Annie.

I smuggle *Little Women* out of the house and hide it behind my math book. I've just got to the part where Jo cuts off all her hair when Mrs. Bottomly catches me. She snaps the book shut and puts it on her desk. Why is she picking on me? At least I'm quiet.

Recess. Twenty lonely minutes, leaning against the wall not skipping. My skipping rope was lost in the fire, so I can't even skip by myself.

There's a tap on my shoulder.

"Hello, Peggy," says Spud.

"Good-bye, Spud."

"Don't be like that. I didn't know it was your house."

"Yes, you did. I told you."

"Well, I couldn't let anyone else get the stuff, could I?"

I'm confused. I don't know what to think. Spud's friendly and fun, but the memory of our burnt-out house and Spud treating it like it was nothing still makes me angry.

"Want to see what I found at your place?"

"If you mean bits of that bomb wing, no thanks."

"It's not that," he says. "It was too stuck. I got other stuff."

"Don't believe you. Everything was burned."

"Suit yourself," says Spud with a shrug. He puts his hands in his pockets, turns his back on me and walks away.

Maybe he did find something.

"Spud, wait." I run round in front of him. "What did you find? If it's from my house, it belongs to me."

"Finders keepers," he says with a grin.

He's so annoying, but I have to see what he found. "Go on, show me."

"Don't be daft. I couldn't bring anything to school. I keep my finds in a secret place."

"Show me after school, then? I promise I won't tell."

Spud looks at me for a long minute. "We could go now," he says.

I have never ever cut school in my whole life, but my curiosity can't wait. "All right."

"Go over to the air-raid shelter and do what I do," he says under his breath.

"What about Mashman?" I whisper back.

"Don't worry about her. She can't see over there."

The air-raid shelter is right next to the school gate. I join up with Spud, and as soon as the duty teacher is looking the other way, Spud nudges me. We sidle out of the playground and run round the corner out of sight of the school.

"You can stop running now," calls Spud, slowing to a walk.

"Don't want to stop," I yell as I overtake him. "I want to run forever."

My feet tap the pavement as I speed along. No one has any petrol, so I don't even look before running across the roads. I run until I can't take another step. Sitting on a low wall, I gulp in air and wait for Spud. He's a long way behind. The sky is a pale winter blue, and a barrage balloon floats above me like a lazy whale.

"Look what I found," he says when he reaches me. In his open hand are some spent bullets. "Two more for my collection."

I roll my eyes.

"Do you often cut school?" I ask as he sits down beside me.

"Done it a few times."

"Did you get into trouble?"

Spud shrugs.

I take it that means yes. I feel a bit funny inside and wonder if Mrs. Bottomly has noticed I'm not in class.

"Cor! Look at that," says Spud. He stands up and points to the barrage balloon. It's moving across the sky.

"Has it broken free?"

"Don't know. Let's find out."

With our eyes locked on the balloon, we fly around the streets, jumping over walls and leaping across potholes. Shouts and orders come from the next street. We turn the corner, and the mystery is solved. Our barrage balloon is attached to a slow-moving army lorry. It's trying hard to escape, but steel wires hold it fast.

"What are you doing with the balloon?" Spud asks one of the women walking beside the lorry.

"Repositioning it to stop the Doodlebugs," she says.

The women are in army uniform. They shout to each other as they pull on ropes and tighten wires.

The balloon is not very cooperative.

"Does your mum do war work, Spud? Mine only does mum-stuff, like looking after Tommy."

"My mum's...Ain't got a mum," he says quickly.

"That's awful." I can't imagine not having a mum. It's bad enough having Dad gone and no home, but no mum—that must be terrible.

"But if I did," he continues, "she'd be driving a lorry."

We walk in silence for a bit. "Where's your hideout?" I ask.

"It's over that way," he says, pointing up a side road. "Come on." Spud takes off at a run, and I race after him. I never guessed today would be so much fun.

"This is a shortcut," says Spud, climbing over a pile of bricks and wood that was once a house. A shiver ripples down my back as we scramble through the rooms. I stop in what must have been the kitchen and look up at the sky.

"Wonder what happened to them?"

"Who?"

"The family that lived in this house."

"You're daft," says Spud, jumping down into the street. "Are you coming or not?"

I catch up to him just as he turns down a back alley.

"Twelve, thirteen, fourteen..." says Spud, banging each plank with a stick.

"What are you doing?"

He ignores me and keeps counting. Then he turns and looks me straight in the eye.

"This is top secret," he says in a low voice. "You've got to swear you won't ever tell."

"Cross my heart and hope to die."

Satisfied, Spud pushes apart two loose planks and squeezes through the gap. I climb after him. On the other side of the fence is a bare allotment smelling of musty leaves and old cabbages. We squelch over to a derelict shed in the far corner.

"My shrapnel collection's in here," says Spud, taking away the piece of wood that pretends to be the door. "What do you think of this lot, then?" He stands back so that I can look in.

The shed is crammed full of rubbish. It's up to the roof in some places. I squint into the darkness hoping like mad there'll be something I recognize. All I see are junk and cobwebs.

"Which bits came from my house?"

"Move out of the way, and I'll show you," says Spud. He steps inside. The walls sway, and the old shed looks like it will collapse on his head at any minute. When he comes out, his arms are full of blackened metal.

"This did and this," he says, laying the pieces on the ground.

I can't believe my eyes. In his hand is my biscuit tin of Dad's letters. It's so black that I can't make out the puppy on the lid, but I'd know it anywhere. I want to laugh and cry and hug him, but all I do is stand there blinking like crazy.

"That's a really special tin. I thought it was gone forever."

"Here, take it," says Spud, handing it to me. "The lid won't come off. Probably got melted on by the fire."

"Doesn't matter."

As I stand there staring at my tin, the hooter sounds at the munitions factory. It's two o'clock. School will be finishing soon. I suddenly realize how much trouble I'm in. My schoolbag, my book and my gas mask are back at school, my shoes are covered in mud, and I can't take my biscuit tin home without explaining how I got it. I feel like a popped balloon.

"What do we do now?"

"Have lunch," says Spud, taking a squished packet from his pocket. He unwraps a Marmite sandwich and gives me half.

"Thanks."

"Then," he continues with his mouth full, "we'll go back to school just as everyone's coming out. It will look like we've been there all day."

I look at him.

"You really have done this before!"

Spud grins and stuffs the rest of his sandwich in his mouth.

"Will you keep my tin for me?"

"If you want," he says and puts it back in the shed.

Chapter 9

It all works out exactly like Spud says. We mingle in as if we'd spent all day in school.

"Bye, Peg," calls Spud.

"See you tomorrow," I call back.

I walk home as slowly as possible. How am I going to explain not having my stuff with me? My stomach churns at the thought of all the trouble I am in. Spud always gets me into trouble. Why did I go with him?

Mum opens the door before I'm even halfway up the path.

"Hi, Peggy. How was school?" She's smiling, and her eyes look bright.

"Same as usual."

Tommy toddles down the hall and jumps into my arms.

"Hello, Tom-Tom. Were you a good boy today?"

"The kettle's on. Hang up your coat, and then I'd like to have a little chat," says Mum.

She must know about me cutting school. I feel awful.

"Where's your bag and your gas mask?"

"I forgot them."

"Oh, Peggy! And look at your dress. How did it get so black?"

"Just playing," I say, looking at the floor and out the window, anywhere but at Mum.

Grandad is in the garden, so there's just us in the back room. Mum hands me a cup of tea and sits down. Her fingers fidget with her apron strings.

I decide to own up about my day off.

"Mum, I..."

"Peggy, I..."

We laugh as we both start talking at the same time.

"You go first, Mum."

"Peggy, I've got a job in the parachute factory, starting tomorrow."

"What!"

"The factory is looking for more workers, and the pay's good."

My mum going out to work again. That's the last thing I expected.

"What about Tommy?" is all I can think to say.

"Mrs. Jones at number six is going to mind him for us. She has two little boys, and Tommy will be able to make as much noise and mess as he wants."

"He'll like that."

"You'll have to pick up Tommy after school and look after him until I get home. You won't mind too much, will you?"

"No. Course I won't."

"Do you think I'm doing the right thing, Peggy? I haven't been out to work since Tommy was born. Maybe it's not such a good idea. I should stay at home."

"Try the job, Mum. I saw some women moving a barrage balloon today. It looked like fun."

"If it works out, maybe soon we'll be able to afford a place of our own, just you, me and Tommy," Mum whispers.

"Really?"

She puts a finger on her lips and nods. We both smile at our secret.

Strange thumps come from behind Grandad's chair.

"What's Tommy doing?"

"Oh, no," cries Mum.

Tommy has pulled all the books off the bottom shelf of Grandad's bookcase.

"Stop that, Tommy," says Mum in her stern voice.

Tommy's face creases up, and he starts bawling. She moves him out of the way while I start putting the books back.

I can hear Grandad stamping the mud off his boots at the back door. I try to put the books away faster.

"Who tromped all that mud through my house?" Grandad bellows.

Oh, no! My muddy shoes.

He storms into the room and stops. His face is bright red.

"What on earth's going on here?"

"I'm sorry about this," says Mum.

"Mind, out the way," says Grandad, stomping over to the bookcase. "Don't you have any respect for other people's belongings?"

Grabbing Tommy round the waist, I run up to my room. The row rises through the floorboards. If I'd stayed in school, my shoes wouldn't be muddy, and the row would only have been half as bad. I hate school, and I hate living here.

"You play on the bed, Tommy. I've got to write to Dad."

Dear Dad

Tommy and I are in the bedroom hiding from another row. Everything we do upsets Grandad. Then Mum gets into trouble. It's not fair.

I wonder how many days Mum will have to work before there's enough money for us to get our own place. I hope it will be back in our old neighborhood so that I can go to my old school with my old friends. I just want everything to be back the way it was.

Love, Peggy

Chapter 10

I'm floating on the ocean, holding a balloon-shaped cloud on a string, when everything starts rocking.

"Peggy! Peggy, wake up." Mum is shaking me. It can't be morning already; I've only just gone to sleep.

"Peggy, get up," says Mum again.

"I'm tired," I whimper and turn over.

"Come on, luv. This is my first day at work. We've got to get a move on. I can't be late."

Before she can say any more, we hear a loud yell from the kitchen.

"Someone come and look after this child," calls Grandad.

Mum leaves me and runs down the stairs. I follow her.

"I thought you agreed last night to keep a better eye on him."

Tommy is grinning from ear to ear. He has tipped his porridge out and is wearing the bowl on his head. I want to laugh, but I don't.

"Oh, Tommy. You naughty boy," sighs Mum. "Get the dishcloth, Peggy. Why is this happening today?"

Between us, Mum and I feed Tommy, get him dressed and clean up the mess. Grandad just stands around grumbling. I don't bother to listen anymore. We'll soon be gone and he can go back to being all by himself in his gloomy house.

Mum closes the front door behind us. "Today has to get better," she says. "It can't possibly get any worse."

I'm not sure about that. I give Tommy a kiss.

"Mm...Mm...Mm..." Tommy blows me back a dozen kisses, grins and waves both hands.

"Bye, Mum. Good luck," I say, although if Mrs. Mashman has found out about me and Spud playing hooky, I'll be the one needing the luck.

"Bye, luv. Don't forget to pick up Tommy."

"I won't."

There's no avoiding Mrs. Mashman. She's standing by the gate.

"Wait outside my office," she booms as soon as I am within hearing range.

Spud's already there, sitting on a bench outside her door. "Hello," he says and slides to the other end to make room for me. He gives me a grin, but it's not a very big grin.

The seat is hard. A lump grows inside me as the hands of the office clock move to the top. How can ten minutes take so long? Then I hear Mrs. Mashman's footsteps and wish for another ten minutes.

"In my office, Peggy Fisher."

I think I'm going to be sick.

The lecture goes on and on. Because I'm new, it's a whole week of detention after school. Starting today. Mrs. Mashman sends me back to class and calls Spud in.

My steps clatter down the corridor and slow as I near the classroom door. I can't stay after school. I have to pick up Tommy. I turn back to the office, my brain searching for the best words to explain the Tommy thing.

Spud is coming out of her office. He's blowing on the palms of his hands.

"You got the strap?"

"Didn't hurt," he says.

I don't believe him. How can I talk to Mrs. Mashman now? She's an ogre.

"I got a week's detention after school, but I have to mind Tommy."

"Wouldn't skip detention if I was you," says Spud, putting on another performance of blowing on his hands.

"What am I going to do?"

We're nearly at my classroom door.

"I could fetch him for you," offers Spud.

"Could you? Oh, I don't know. Last time I left Tommy with someone else, my Mum was really angry."

"I'll pick him up and come back to meet you. No one will know."

I like Spud. If only he wasn't always getting into trouble. I don't know what to do.

"Okay," I say reluctantly. I have no choice. "Remember to clip him into his pram, then come straight back here. Promise you won't go anywhere else."

"I promise, I promise."

"It'll just be for today. I'll sort something out for tomorrow." I don't know what though.

My cutting school has a strange effect on the rest of the class. Suddenly I'm not invisible. Annie says hello and shows me where we are up to in our English book.

"You're dead brave taking off like that. I'd never have the nerve," she whispers.

The girl behind taps me on the shoulder and gives me her spare pencil. "My name's Doreen," she says. "I bet Mashman gave it to you."

"I'm never ever doing it again," I tell her firmly.

At recess, Elsie asks me to come and join in the skipping.

Spud gives me a wave from the other side of the playground. I'd go over and talk to him, but it's my turn to jump in.

School is over. Only Mrs. Bottomly and I are left in the classroom. I go over to the blackboard and pick up a piece of chalk. Mrs. Bottomly smiles at me.

"Best get started, dear," she says. She doesn't seem to mind that I have made her stay late too.

I write I MUST NOT LEAVE THE SCHOOL PREMISES WITHOUT PERMISSION on the board. Then I write it again underneath. With every line, my worry about Tommy grows. Whatever was I thinking? Mrs. Jones isn't going to give Tommy to some strange boy. By the time I reach the bottom of the board, two fat tears have rolled down my cheeks.

"A few lines are nothing to cry about," says Mrs. Bottomly.

"It's not the lines," I sob. "I was meant

to pick up my baby brother after school. Spud says he'll get Tommy and come and meet me. But he doesn't know Tommy, and Mrs. Jones doesn't know Spud."

I'm sure Mrs. Bottomly doesn't know what I'm going on about, but she stands up and takes the chalk out of my hand. "Go fetch your brother," she says. "You can do your lines in the lunch hour."

"Oh, thank you, Mrs. Bottomly."

"You only had to ask, dear," she says. "Now off you go."

Still sniffing, I grab my coat, my bag, my gas mask and run as fast as I can out of the school, across the playground, over the road, round the corner, on and on. I arrive at Mrs. Jones' house just as she's opening the door to Spud. She looks surprised to see Spud standing there, but smiles when she sees me running up the path.

"Sorry I'm late, Mrs. Jones," I pant. "This is my friend Spud."

Before our introductions are complete, Tommy comes bouncing down the hall and leaps into my arms.

"Bin as good as gold," says Mrs. Jones. She buttons up Tommy's coat and helps me strap him into the pram. "See you tomorrow, darlin'." Tommy blows his good-bye kisses, and we turn to go.

"Thought I was picking him up," says Spud.

"Bottomly says I can write the lines in the lunch hour."

"Oh."

"Thanks for helping me out and everything."

"That's okay," says Spud.

"We could do something. As long as we take Tommy along."

"Naw," says Spud. "Don't really like babies." He puts his hands in his pockets and walks off.

The late-afternoon sun pokes through the clouds as I push Tommy home. Today wasn't nearly as bad as I imagined. Grandad is in a good mood, and when Mum comes in I can tell by her face that making parachutes is a lot more fun than staying at home with Grandad.

"Are you asleep?" she asks softly when we are both in bed.

"Not yet."

"I fold the parachutes," she says. "It's awfully important to do it right."

"Is it?" I'm too sleepy to talk.

"The other girls are ever so nice."

I drift off to sleep listening to the contented purr of Mum's voice as she talks about her day in the factory.

Dear Dad

Mum loves her job. But there's such a hullabaloo in the mornings that Grandad has decided to stay in bed until we are all out of the house.

Straight after school I pick up Tommy and look after him until Mum gets home. I don't mind. It's not like I have a best friend. Well, not one who lives near. I like Annie, but she's best friends with Doreen. Spud's fun too, but you can't be best friends with a boy. I'm glad Mum's happy, but I do miss our after-school chats.

Love, Peggy

Chapter 11

It's Friday at last. The afternoon bell rings just as I am writing my five hundredth I MUST NOT LEAVE THE SCHOOL PREMISES WITHOUT PERMISSION. I put the chalk down and smile at Mrs. Bottomly. We've almost become friends during the week. I've told her all about Tommy, Mum's job and how hard it is living in Grandad's house. Her son is in the Navy, just like Dad, but he's lost at sea. Did Dad get lost?

"Five hundred boring lines. I wish Mrs. Mashman had given me something interesting to write about."

"Such as?" asks Mrs. Bottomly.

"Oh, I don't know, anything."

"I used to write a few articles for a small newspaper," says Mrs. Bottomly, blushing slightly.

"Did you?" I'm surprised. I can't picture Mrs. Bottomly doing something exciting like being a reporter.

"I was much younger of course, but it was so much fun." She walks over to the blackboard, picks up the eraser and starts cleaning the board. Puffs of chalk dust dance in the sunlight streams.

"Why did you stop?"

"Being a teacher was a more appropriate job for a woman. I never liked teaching though. Only came back because there is such a shortage of teachers with everyone doing war work."

"I think it's a shame that you couldn't do what you wanted."

Mrs. Bottomly smiles at me. "I know, dear, but times are changing for women."

The rest of the class pours in. I take my seat, ready for another noisy afternoon.

"I wonder what mood Grandad's in today," I say to Tommy on the way home after school. I lift him onto the ground and bump the pram into the shed. Before I can close the shed door, Tommy's taken off up the garden path.

"Come back here, little rascal." Tommy looks back, waiting for me to chase him. He bursts into giggles when I catch him.

"Hello, Grandad," I call from the back door. "Any letters for me today?" There never are, but I always ask.

"On the hall table," says Grandad. "Don't forget to wipe your shoes on the mat."

"There is a letter!" My heart misses a beat as I pick up the envelope. I immediately recognize Nora's handwriting.

"Thanks, Grandad!" I give him a kiss, which I haven't done since I was little.

He smiles and takes Tommy's hand. "You come along with me, young fellow. Your sister's got a letter to read."

I take the stairs two at a time, climb over to my bed, get comfy against the wall and open my letter. My eyes prickle as I read about all the goings-on in my old school. It seems so long ago that I sat in my desk next to Nora, passing notes and planning what to do at the weekend.

Strange Tommy noises are seeping through the floorboards. I tuck the letter under my pillow and go downstairs to investigate.

Tommy is sitting on Grandad's knee, and they're both growling at a picture of a tiger in a wild animal book. Grandad turns the page, and the growl changes to a roar.

"Can I join in?" I growl. Tommy shakes his tiny claws at me, and Grandad laughs a deep hearty laugh. I think he's beginning to like having us around.

"Time to peel some potatoes," says Grandad, closing the book. "I spent two hours queuing for some minced beef this morning. Thought we'd make a shepherd's pie for our tea. Make a change from Spam."

There's not much meat. The shepherd's pie is nearly all potatoes and onions, but it smells good bubbling away in the oven.

I can't wait for Mum to get home so that I can show her my letter.

We hear the key turn in the lock, and I follow a giggly tiger to the front door.

"Mum…" I say, but the rest of my sentence vanishes. Mum is wearing a pair of dark blue trousers. They look just like a man's.

"What on earth have you got on?" thunders Grandad from the kitchen door.

"Lots of women wear trousers these days," says Mum. Her voice wavers. "They are much more practical than working in a dress."

Grandad doesn't listen. He turns his back on Mum and stomps off to the kitchen. His happy mood has vanished.

"What do you think, Peggy?" asks Mum.

"I think you've spoilt everything. We were getting along fine until you came home." I push past her to the stairs, stamp up to the bedroom and slam the door.

Just when it's beginning to feel like home, everything gets ruined. I look at the *Home Is Where the Heart Is* sampler on the wall. My heart is definitely not here. Why did Mum have to go and make Grandad angry? And why is Grandad always bossing Mum about? I'm mad at both of them.

Tears try to squeeze out of my eyes, but I blink them away. I'm not going to cry. And I'm not going downstairs. A hungry growl gurgles round my stomach. And I'm not going to eat my tea, even if Mum brings it up to me on a tray. In fact, I'm never going to talk to either of them ever again. It's all the fault of those stupid trousers.

Suddenly I want to laugh. I imagine the trousers standing at the blackboard writing I MUST NOT UPSET THE FISHER FAMILY one hundred times. I'm sure Dad wouldn't mind Mum wearing trousers. He'd like her whatever she wore.

I hear Mum's footsteps on the stairs. She comes into the bedroom. Her face looks sad as she takes off the trousers and puts on a skirt.

"Mum."

She glances over at me.

"Aren't you going to wear your trousers anymore?"

"Of course I am," she says defiantly. "Everything is changing, Peggy, and women are changing faster than anything else."

Funny, that's what Mrs. Bottomly said.

"I'm sorry, Mum. You look really nice in trousers." We hug and make up.

"Want to see my letter from Nora?"

"Christmas in two weeks!" she exclaims as she reads the letter. "There's been so much going on I've lost track of the days."

"Can I visit Nora, Mum? Oh, please say yes."

"We'll see."

Dear Dad
Some days are good, and some days are bad. But everything is changing. Sometimes the whole world seems upside down. Mum goes out to work, and Grandad

stays at home doing the shopping and cooking. He complains that the queues for food are getting longer, but I think he likes chatting to everybody while he waits to be served. He's not a bad cook, but we do have a lot of Spam fritters and fish paste sandwiches. All the vegetables he grew in his Victory garden are gone. If we hadn't been staying here they would have lasted him all winter.

I just want two things for Christmas: a pair of trousers and a visit from Nora.

Love, Peggy

Chapter 12

As we take out our books on Monday morning, the dreaded footsteps come tapping down the corridor.

"It's Mashman," warns Annie, madly opening her books.

The boys in the back row jump into their seats just as the door flies open. Mrs. Mashman marches in, followed by three girls and Spud. "We're going to have to make do with one less teacher, Mrs. Bottomly, so I'm changing the classes round again. Here are four new pupils for you: Stanley, Thelma, Ivy and Alice."

Spud holds two fingers up behind Thelma's head, giving her rabbit's ears.

The class titters. Mrs. Mashman spins round, but Spud's too quick for her. The ears have disappeared into his pocket.

With a parting glare that freezes everyone in their seats, Mrs. Mashman turns and leaves the room.

"Can you imagine having her for your mother?" says Doreen. Annie and I shudder.

Mrs. Bottomly assigns the new kids their seats, stands up and bangs her desk with a ruler. "From now until the end of term, we're going to do something different. Peggy gave me the idea."

I did?

"What idea?" mouths Annie.

"Don't know."

"We're all going to be reporters," continues Mrs. Bottomly, unrolling a large sheet of paper.

"Where did she get all that paper," whispers Doreen from behind. "I thought paper was in short supply, and that's not even utility paper."

"Sshhh," I say. "I want to be a reporter."

"This paper is going to be our newspaper. It's going to be divided into columns. Each of you can write a true story about your family and the things that are going on around you.

"Now who would like to be our editor?"

"Sounds like extra work to me," whispers Doreen.

I like the idea, but before my hand is all the way up, Spud shoots his into the air. I didn't know he was keen on writing.

"Well, Stanley and Peggy, you can both be our editors." Spud gives me a wink.

What have I let myself in for?

"Let's talk about what we're going to write about. You must all have lots of stories."

Doreen puts her hand up. "I haven't got any stories, Miss."

"Goodness me, child," says Mrs. Bottomly. "Look around you. Just being in London in 1944 makes you part of history." She walks into the center of the classroom and waves her sheet of paper. "Just think, everyone, this newspaper could become a historic document."

I'm part of history? The words buzz round my head. That makes me as important as any king or queen.

"Tom, you start us off. Stand up and tell us something about yourself or your family," says Mrs. Bottomly.

"I've got 132 spent bullet cases," says Tom.

Another boy gives him a shove. "No you 'aven't," he says. "Half of them's mine."

The room erupts into a shrapnel shouting match. I lean back in my chair. I knew the class-newspaper idea was too good to be true.

"QUIET!"

Everyone stops talking and looks up at Spud, who is standing on his desk.

"Thank you, Stanley," says Mrs. Bottomly. "You can sit down now."

"I'm the editor, so I get to keep everyone in order."

Mrs. Bottomly flutters her hands. "I don't know about that, dear. Umm...Let's continue."

She points to Elsie in the front row.

"My story is going to be about how our chimney was blown off by a bomb," she says.

"That's exactly the sort of story we need in our newspaper. Very good, dear...Now, Thelma."

"My cousins were evacuated to Canada at the beginning of the war. Mum wouldn't let me go. She wanted us all to stay together. I wonder if I'll ever see them again."

George sticks his hand up. "Miss, Miss," he says before Thelma has finished talking. "My brother lied about his age just so that he could be a pilot and fly Spitfires. Dad is so furious he won't talk to him."

"That's what I'm going to do when I'm old enough," says Fred. "I'm going to get into dogfights and shoot down enemy planes." He gives a demonstration with loud sound effects. George joins in. Why do boys always act like little kids?

"Come in to land, Fred and George," says Mrs. Bottomly. For the first time since I've been in this class, everyone's paying attention.

"You're next, Pete."

"When it rains our Anderson shelter floods, and one day my uncle forgot and fell in." Everyone bursts out laughing.

Dora's story isn't funny. Her dad is missing. He might be in a prisoner-of-war camp. I'm glad my dad's not a prisoner. He would hate that.

Suddenly everyone has a story. The classroom is a forest of waving arms, all wanting to be next.

Is my story going to be about Dad's ship escorting a convoy from Halifax or our house burning down? No, those stories are not for sharing. I'll stick to Mum folding parachutes.

Mrs. Bottomly points to Spud. "You're next, Stanley."

He scrapes his chair back and stands up. "I thought I just had to paste the stories on the newspaper."

"You have to write one too," she says.

"Oh!" groans Spud.

"Tell us about your family," encourages Mrs. Bottomly.

I suddenly realize how little I know about Spud.

Spud runs his hand through his hair. The rest of the class fidgets.

"My mum drives a lorry and moves barrage balloons around," he says with a grin.

I can't believe my ears.

"That's an interesting story, Spud," says Mrs. Bottomly, raising her eyebrows.

It's not an interesting story; it's a fairy story. Is he lying because he doesn't want everyone to feel sorry for him?

"Peggy." Mrs. Bottomly points to me, but before I can get to my feet, the chilling notes of the air-raid siren set the class into motion.

"Quick as you can, boys and girls."

We all know what to do because of Mrs. Mashman's daily drills, but my legs still tremble as I grab my gas mask.

"Lead the way, Tom," says Mrs. Bottomly.

We file across the playground and down the steep steps into the air-raid shelter.

Two wooden benches run along each wall of the tunnel-shaped underground room. It smells of old socks, and we have to squish up really tight to get all the classes in.

Elsie starts crying. "Air raids are so scary. I wish I lived in the country," she sobs.

"Oh no, you don't," says Doreen. "I was evacuated to a farm in Devon. It was full of enormous, smelly cows. I was so scared me Mum had to come and fetch me home."

"Don't believe you," says Annie.

"It's true."

"Quiet, everyone," says Mrs. Mashman, clapping her hands. "Stop sniveling, Elsie." She looks at her watch. "We cut one minute, twenty-nine seconds from yesterday's drill. Well done, school. Now let's begin our multiplication tables. We'll start with sevens."

As planes drone overhead, we chant the familiar numbers in our singsongy voices. I think about the barrage balloon in its new position and then I don't feel quite so scared.

Chapter 13

School is dismissed as soon as the all-clear sounds. We have the whole afternoon off. Doreen wants all the girls to go down the high street and look round Woolworth's. It feels great to be included, but I want to talk to Spud. He's nowhere around. Must have raced off. I bet he's gone to his hut. I decide to go over to the allotment and find out once and for all. Has he got a mum or hasn't he?

Before I get to the sliding planks, I hear loud voices coming from the allotment. Squatting down, I peer through a knothole. Two men wearing Home Guard armbands are stomping round Spud's hut.

"It's goin' to have to come down, Fred," says the tall one.

"If it don't fall down first," laughs the other, holding the door in his hand. "Cor blimey, look at all the scrap metal!"

My biscuit box of letters is not scrap metal. I keep listening. This is awful.

"What you doing, Peg?" Spud appears out of nowhere, making me jump out of my skin.

"Ssshhh. Look. They're going to take away your hut and everything in it."

"They're not getting my shrapnel," he says.

I grab his jacket to stop him from racing over to them.

"Keep still. They'll see us."

"Took me ages to collect that lot," mutters Spud.

"We'll need the large barrow," says Fred.

"It's back at my house," says the tall one. "Come on, we'll get the missus to make us a cuppa while we're there." They tramp over to the gate and leave the allotments.

"We're going to have to move everything before they come back, Spud."

"Where to?" he says.

"Your house?" I suggest.

"Mum won't let me."

"Thought you didn't have a mum."

"I don't," says Spud quickly. "I've, er, got a stepmum."

"She must be the one that moves barrage balloons around?"

Spud scowls and disappears into his hut without answering me. I caught him out. He does have a mum. But what's wrong with her? He stomps out with my biscuit tin.

"Here," he says. "You keep it."

I take the tin from him. Thank goodness Dad's letters are safe. Suddenly I get an idea.

"We could put your shrapnel in my Grandad's toolshed."

"Will he let us?" asks Spud.

"It'll only be till we find somewhere else. Grandad won't be doing any more gardening till spring."

91

"That's brilliant," says Spud, a smile back on his face. He dives into the hut and comes out with a piece of metal in each hand.

"This is part of a bomber. It was lying on our shed one morning, and this is a..."

"Spud, we don't have time for the story of every piece. Fred and his mate will be back soon. Just put the pieces you want to keep over here, and be quick."

The "keeper pile" grows larger and larger.

"Stop. We can't carry all that."

"We'll use your old pram to move it," says Spud.

If I hadn't been holding the biscuit tin of Dad's letters I'd have said no, but special things are special things.

"Okay."

"Let's go and get it," says Spud.

It's beginning to rain as we reach Mrs. Jones' house.

"Crouch down, Spud. If Tommy sees me, he'll want to come."

We creep up to the pram, which is standing outside the front door. The brake sticks, as usual, and I need both hands to free it.

Suddenly the front door opens.

"Oh, there you are, dear," says Mrs. Jones. "I was just going to bring the pram in out of the rain. You're nice and early today."

"Hello, Mrs. Jones. I've..."

"I'll just go and get Tommy," she says.

"No. No, it's all right. He can stay a little longer."

Mrs. Jones isn't listening. She turns down the hall.

"We just want to borrow the pram for half an hour," I say to her back.

"TOM-MEE! Your sister's here," she booms at the top of her voice. Her boys come racing down the hallway, followed by little Tommy. He's one big smile when he sees me.

"Here's his coat," says Mrs. Jones.

"He'll have to come with us, Spud. He's no trouble, honestly."

"There won't be enough room for my shrapnel," grumbles Spud.

"We'll do two trips."

Spud is still complaining as I clip Tommy into the pram and only shuts up when I threaten to go home.

It's raining harder now, but Tommy is safe and dry sitting under the hood. Spud runs ahead to see if anyone's at the allotment.

"All clear," he yells. "Come on."

It's hard pushing through the mud, and Spud has to lift the front of the pram to get it out of a rut. Luckily there's still no sign of Fred.

As fast as he can, Spud hands me the pieces of shrapnel. I fill the shopping basket on the back of the pram, then pack other pieces in blankets along the side and around Tommy's feet.

Tommy thinks it's a great game. With hoots of giggles he picks up anything within reach and drops it over the side.

"Stop it, Tommy." He's getting dirty and wet. I'm getting dirty and wet. How am I going to explain all this? There's going to be another row. I know there is.

"Spud, that's enough. It's going to be too heavy to push."

"Just one more bit," he says and hands me a thing that looks like a baked-bean tin with wings. It just fits on top of the pile.

"That's it. Let's go."

Spud heaves on the front, and I push on the handle until the pram is through the mud and on the road. Rain is bouncing off the pavement, and Tommy is beginning to whine.

"Let's hurry. I'm getting soaked." I'm also beginning to wish I hadn't suggested Grandad's shed. I could be at home, warm and dry.

We walk faster. Rain is running down my hair into my eyes, and I can hardly see where I'm going. Nearly there. Just have to pass the bombed-out post office and turn up our road.

Looking up, I see a man limping toward the pram.

"Grandad!"

He comes up to the pram.

"Peggy! What on earth? Stand back, both of you!" Grabbing my arm, he yanks me away from the pram. He points to the winged tin can.

"That's a bomb!" he yells.

Chapter 14

My whole body goes tight, and for a moment I can't move. My baby brother is sitting in a pram next to an unexploded bomb, and I'm the one who put it there.

Tommy is struggling to get out. He doesn't understand what's going on, but he's frightened just the same.

"Let go of me, Grandad. We can't leave Tommy sitting there."

"Stay back. I'll get him," orders Grandad.

He goes to the pram and pulls at Tommy. He doesn't know anything about prams and baby things.

"Grandad, he's strapped in. Let me do it. I've unclipped him hundreds of times."

Grandad steps aside "Be very very careful," he says. As if I need telling.

"Up, up," demands Tommy.

"I know, Tom-Tom. Soon have you out." He needs a hug, but there's no time. The clip is buried under the shrapnel.

"Let's sing a song, Tommy."

"We haven't time for any songs," yells Grandad.

"It's raining, it's pouring, the old man is snoring," I sing in a crackly voice.

The hood is going to have to come down even though Tommy will get soaked. He's cold, and now he's going to be wet. The singing doesn't help. His whimpers turn to loud yells.

"Get rid of this, Spud." I hand him a piece of shrapnel, and he throws it down the dip that was once a post office.

"Be careful," yells Grandad again. "We don't know what kind of fuse is in that thing. It could go off any minute."

One by one, without jogging the main

pile, I pass out bits of metal from the side of the pram.

"Don't cry, Tommy. Not long now."

At last the clip is clear. My fingers are wet and slippery, and they won't stop shaking. I push and push with all my strength, but the clip won't open.

"Hurry," yells Spud.

"It's jammed. It won't move. Spud, try the other one."

Tommy is bawling louder than ever. Grandad is telling me to be careful for the millionth time, and Spud is yelling too.

I can't think.

"You're doing good, girl," says Grandad softly.

My heart is pumping so hard I can hardly breathe. Stay calm, I keep telling myself.

"Stuck, stuck," cries Tommy.

"I know, Tommy. I know."

Suddenly I remember watching Dad free a rusty bolt. Instead of pulling, he jiggled it sideways. I try the same thing, moving the clip back and forth, back and forth. I can feel it loosening under my fingers. Another wiggle, a hard squeeze and the clip opens.

"This one's free."

"I can't find the clip," calls Spud from the other side of the pram.

Leaning over Tommy, I slide my hand along. Where is it?

"Tom-Tom, up," cries Tommy. "Up, up, up." He stretches his little arms toward me, and as he moves the clip appears.

"There it is!" screams Spud.

Luckily this clip is easier than the first. One hard push and the harness is free.

"Let's go, Tommy."

He climbs into my arms and we race over to Grandad.

Spud gives the pram a mighty push. It bounces down into the bombsite, hits a wooden beam, turns over and explodes.

There's a crack like thunder and a flash like lightning, but no storm has ever been this scary. The ground shakes, and the rain quivers.

Grandad throws us to the ground and stretches his arms and coat over our heads. His heart is beating louder than mine. Bricks and metal clatter down around us.

Then it's quiet. There's just the sound of the rain.

Tommy wriggles underneath me, and Grandad moves his arm.

"Is everyone all right?" he asks.

Slowly I raise my head. Through a curtain of rain and smoke, I see a pram wheel. It's still turning. There's a piece of pram handle on the pavement, and part of Tommy's blanket has fallen near my hand. The pram is completely destroyed.

Spud lies motionless on the ground. I scramble over to him.

"Spud! Don't be hurt. Please be all right."

He slowly rolls over. There's pain on his face, but it turns to a grin when he sees me. "What a bang!" he says.

I pound on his chest.

"This isn't a game. You nearly killed my brother. You nearly killed me."

Grandad pulls me away.

"It's okay, luv. It's all over. Everyone's safe."

Grandad looks like he's crying, but it may be the rain.

"I don't know what I'd have done if I had lost you two as well," he says.

"You mean you'd miss us?"

"Very much," says Grandad. I put my arms around him. His clothes smell of his favorite tobacco, his voice is low and his arms are big enough for Tommy and me.

Suddenly people are all around us.

"Let's get you folks checked over at the hospital," says a policeman, putting a blanket round my shoulders. As I glance back over the scene, I realize that Dad's letters are gone for good.

Chapter 15

Tommy shows off his bandaged knee to everyone who passes as the nurse finishes stitching the cut on my arm. My clothes were soaked right through to my underwear so I'm wearing a hospital gown, but I can't stop shaking, even in a warm room with a blanket round my shoulders.

"Where's Spud. Is he okay?"

"Cuts, bruises and a broken arm. Bit shaken up too," says the nurse. "He's in the next cubicle. I've sent for his mother."

"We'll stay with him until she comes," says Grandad.

The nurse finishes with me and pulls aside the curtain. Spud's face is as white as the sheets.

"You don't have to stay," he says.

"Of course we'll stay."

He lies back on the pillow, too exhausted to argue.

The door opens. Mum rushes in and surrounds me in a hug that lasts forever. She touches my head and inspects my arms and hands while Grandad recounts the adventure. He makes Spud and me sound like heroes, but how can we be heroes when it's all our fault?

The door opens again, and in walks Mrs. Mashman.

What's she doing here?

Mrs. Mashman goes straight to Spud's bed. "Stanley," she says, "what have you been up to this time?"

I look at their matching ginger curls.

"Mashman! Mash potatoes. That's why you're called Spud."

Spud gives me a coy grin from under his mother's hug.

"Time we were going," says Grandad.

Behind a screen, Mum helps me change into the dry clothes she's brought. Then we leave. "Bye, Mrs. Mashman. Bye, Spud. Get well soon."

"You too," they call back.

Dear Dad

The "what ifs" won't go away. They fill my dreams and burst in on my thoughts whatever I'm doing. If anything had happened to Tommy, it would have been all my fault. From now on I'm going to be the best big sister a brother could have.

Grandad was strong and warm and kind. How could I have not liked him? Mrs. Mashman is nice too, when she's not being a headmistress. I'm annoyed at Spud for not telling me the truth about his mum, but I understand. It must be awful hearing people call your mum names every day. My New Year's resolution is to get to know people properly.

Love, Peggy

Chapter 16

"What we used to call a pea souper," says Grandad, joining me at the window. "The good thing is they won't be bombing us and we won't be bombing them today."

The fog outside is thick and yellow. All I can see are murky shapes. They fill my head.

There's just Grandad and me at home. Mum thought we needed some peace and quiet so she took Tommy to Mrs. Jones'. I'm bored, but I don't feel like doing anything. I'm tired, but I'm not sleepy. Grandad seems to understand. Perhaps he's feeling the same way.

"I've got an idea," he says at last. "Come on, Peggy, into the kitchen."

Grandad brings out a large tin and puts it on the table. Inside are paper packets of raisins and currants. There's sugar too.

"I've been saving up my rations. I was going to ask your mother to bake us a Christmas cake. She's a busy woman these days, so why don't we make it?"

"Have you ever made a Christmas cake, Grandad?"

"No, have you?"

"I always make the icing look like snowy footprints and put the fir trees and the little church on top, but Mum bakes the cake."

"Oh," says Grandad. "Never mind. I have your grandma's recipe book. Her cakes were the best."

Grandad fetches the book and shuffles through the pieces of paper stuffed in between the pages. "Here's your grandmother's recipe," he says, handing me an ancient scrap of paper with torn edges and faded writing.

"It's very hard to read, Grandad. It says we need twelve eggs. That's a whole month's ration of egg powder."

"We'll have to adapt it a bit."

The recipe needs a lot of adapting, but as I sieve and stir and mix and pour, the fog disappears from my head.

"Time for a wish," says Grandad, handing me the wooden mixing spoon.

"Can I wish for impossible things?"

Grandad hesitates. "Yes," he says. "But you can't un-wish things. Once something has happened, nothing can change it."

I sigh for a wish that can't be wished, close my eyes, stir the cake three times and wish for Tommy to find a train at the bottom of his bed on Christmas morning. To make up for yesterday.

"Your turn, Grandad."

He takes the spoon, stirs and wishes.

"That was a quick wish, Grandad."

"I just wished for peac—"

I clap my hands over my ears. "Don't tell me, or it won't come true."

He laughs and puts the cake in the oven.

"It's going to take four hours to cook," says Grandad. "We could put up some decorations while we wait. That is, if I can remember where I put the box. This house hasn't celebrated Christmas in years."

He goes up to his room and comes down a while later with a dusty cardboard box.

"Decorate away," he says. "Pin them up wherever you like. I'll just sit here and watch."

The decorations are old and faded, not bright like ours used to be. I stand on a chair and twist streamers along the picture rail. I loop paper chains around the doors. By the time I get to the concertina bells, a warm spicy smell is filling the house.

"Oh, Grandad, it's so Christmasy!"

"You've done a good job, luv," he says. "You've cheered this house up in more ways than one."

There's a knock on the door.

It's Mrs. Mashman and Spud, with his arm in a sling.

"Good afternoon, Peggy," she says. "Stanley has something to say to you." She gives him a nudge. "Go on, Stanley."

"Er...I'm sorry about nearly blowing you and Tommy up," he says. Then he groans under his breath. "I'm not allowed to touch another piece of shrapnel as long as I live."

"It was half my fault," I say. "We're all okay. That's the main thing."

Grandad comes into the hall, and I introduce him to Mrs. Mashman.

"Something smells awfully good," she says.

"I do believe it's our Christmas cake trying to get out of the oven," jokes Grandad. "Come through to the kitchen."

Grandad finds the oven mitts, while I clear a space. A mouthwatering smell fills the kitchen as he opens the oven door. The cake is golden-brown and has risen to the top of the pan. It looks perfect.

"Stand clear, everyone," says Grandad,

swinging the cake out of the oven and onto the table. He stands back. And right in front of our eyes, the beautiful Christmas cake sinks in the middle.

"Looks like a bomb hit it," says Spud with a laugh. Mrs. Mashman scowls at him but can't keep a straight face and clamps her hand over her mouth to keep a laugh in.

Grandad and I stare at the disaster.

"Oh no! We've wasted all that fruit. What's Mum going to say about us using up all the egg and milk rations?"

"She'll skin us alive," says Grandad.

We look at each other and splutter into laughter. It does look a funny sight.

"You must have got your proportions wrong," says Mrs. Mashman. "Never mind, get me a basin and a sixpenny piece."

Grandad frowns but gives her what she needs. She breaks up the warm cake with a fork, pops the sixpence in the middle and pats it firmly into the basin. "You might not have a Christmas cake this year, but you will have a Christmas pudding."

"Bravo, Mrs. Mashman," Grandad says.

"Everyone makes mistakes," she declares, wiping her hands on the dish-cloth. "The important thing is putting things right again."

She gives me a wink and hands me a dish of warm curranty cake crumbs to share with Spud.

"I have the best adventures when I'm with you," mumbles Spud through a mouth full of crumbs.

I roll my eyes and smile. "I just seem to get into trouble when I'm with you."

Dear Dad

Our first Christmas without you is over. Grandad said we'd be having roast pigeon for Christmas dinner, but he was teasing. He bought us a turkey, although we weren't allowed to ask any questions. Tommy found a beautiful wooden train (made by Grandad) by his bed on Christmas morning, and I found a skipping rope—no trousers though. I also won the sixpence in the Christmas pudding, so I'm in for a lucky year. I had another treat too. Nora came to visit for a whole day.

The best surprise of all was from Mum. She gave me a parcel, tied with a big red bow, just before I went to bed on Christmas night. Inside was my battered old biscuit tin full of your last letters. I had left it on the doorstep at Mrs. Jones' house that terrible afternoon. It didn't get destroyed with the pram after all. I was so happy we both cried.

It's nearly a year since Mum got the telegram telling us that a torpedo sank your ship. I used to imagine you swimming home to us, getting a little nearer every day, but I know you will never come home.

I tell Tommy all about you. Especially how much you love the sea and ships.

I didn't believe that this little house by the railway would ever feel like home, but it does. I didn't believe that Grandad, Mum, Tommy and I could make a family, but we do.

I don't need to write to you anymore, but I'm going to anyway. Even when my hair is as white as Mrs. Bottomly's.

Mum's calling. I've got to run.

Keddy's has sausages.

Lots of love always,
Peggy

Glossary

Some words and terms in this story may be unfamiliar.

Allotments: Community garden plots for growing vegetables.

Anderson shelter: A family air-raid shelter. It was dug into the ground and had a semi-circular corrugated metal roof.

Barrage balloons: Hot-air blimps. Their purpose was to stop enemy planes from flying low over large cities.

Blackouts: Thick black curtains or shutters put up at night to keep light from showing outside. Lights would give away the position of towns and cities to enemy aircraft.

The Blitz: A period of sustained and intensive bombing raids on London.

Doodlebug: The nickname given to the V1 rocket. These unmanned rocket bombs were launched from the coast of occupied France in 1944. About half a million homes were destroyed by Doodlebugs, and many Londoners lost their lives.

Headmistress: School principal.

Lav: Toilet.

Marmite: A thick, strong-tasting savory spread.

Nappy: Diaper.

Nicking: A slang word for stealing.

Petrol: Gasoline.

Postman: Letter carrier.

Pram: Baby carriage.

Queue: Line-up.

Rationing: Basic foods were rationed so that everyone, rich or poor, had enough to eat. As the war continued, more foods were added to the ration list.

Shrapnel: Pieces of metal debris from bombs or aircraft.

Sixpence: A small silver coin about the size of a dime.

Tea: The family evening meal.

Jacqueline Halsey grew up in England. As a young adult she lived for five years in a sugar mill village in Natal, South Africa. In recent years, as she watched images of war on television, she realized that her mother and older brother were living in a war zone in London back in the '40s. *Peggy's Letters* is her way of weaving her mother's wartime memories into a book for today's children. Jacqueline lives in Beaver Bank, Nova Scotia.

Orca Young Readers

Orca Young Readers Series

Max and Ellie series by Becky Citra
*Ellie's New Home, The Freezing Moon,
Danger at The Landings, Runaway,
Strawberry Moon*

TJ series by Hazel Hutchins
*TJ and the Cats, TJ and the Haunted House,
TJ and the Rockets*

Basketball series by Eric Walters
*Three on Three, Full Court Press, Hoop Crazy!
Long Shot, Road Trip, Off Season, Underdog,
Triple Threat*

Kaylee and Sausage series by Anita Daher
*Flight from Big Tangle,
Flight from Bear Canyon*